THE LION, THE WITCH AND THE WARDROBE

Peter's Destiny

The Battle for Narnia

THE CHRONICLES OF NARNIA

THE LION, THE WITCH AND THE WARDROBE

Peter's Destiny
The Battle for Narnia

Adapted by Craig Graham

HarperCollins*Publishers*

Lantern Waste

witch's castle

E

mr. tumnus

n

a

the lamp-post

beaver's dam

the great river

the wardrobe

allies' enclave

rock bridge

R

Western Woods

Frozen Lake

cauldron pool

father christmas

shuddering wood

telmar river

archen river

NARNIA

mt. pire

a

NARNIA®

Library of Congress catalog card number: 2005931867
ISBN-10: 0-06-085235-6 (pbk.) — ISBN-13: 978-0-06-085235-1 (pbk.)
ISBN-10: 0-06-085236-4 (trade bdg.) — ISBN-13: 978-0-06-085236-8 (trade bdg.)

❖

Contents

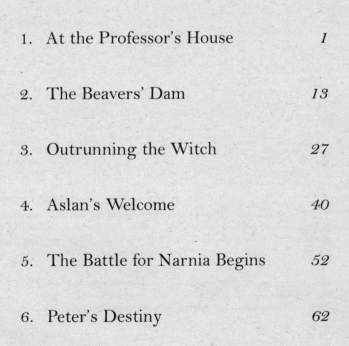

CHAPTER ONE

At the Professor's House

Peter Pevensie tried his best to look interested.

"Come on, Peter," said Susan, his sister. She was holding an open dictionary. "Gastrovascular."

"Is it Latin?" asked his brother, Edmund, stifling a yawn. "For 'worst game ever invented'?"

Susan shut the dictionary with a thump.

"We could play hide-and-seek," said Lucy, the youngest.

"But we're already having so much fun." Peter sighed.

"Hide-and-seek's for children," Edmund added.

Lucy jumped to her feet.

"Come on, Peter!" she cried. "Please?"

Peter sighed again, then covered his eyes.

"One, two, three, four . . ."

As he counted, Peter thought about how he and his brother and sisters had come to be here, miles from home and living with people they didn't even know. Air raids had made London a dangerous place, so many of the city's children were evacuated to the country. Peter's mother had taken them to the railway station with their luggage and boarded them onto a train.

"Promise me you'll look after the others," she

had said to Peter, tears in her eyes.

"I will, Mum," he said, hugging her.

The house they were staying in belonged to Professor Kirke. It was a big, old mansion with stained glass windows. The Professor lived alone, except for his housekeeper, Mrs. Macready, so there was plenty of room for them all. They hadn't seen the Professor yet, as he was always working, but Mrs. Macready seemed a little grumpy. She had already warned them against shouting, running, sliding down the banisters and touching the Professor's things.

"Ninety-nine, one hundred. Ready or not, here I come!"

Peter opened his eyes. No one was in the room. He stepped out into the hall.

"It's all right!" cried Lucy, bursting out of a big wardrobe. "I'm back!"

Edmund stuck his head out from behind a curtain. "Shut up! He's coming."

3

"I'm not sure you two have quite got the idea of this game!" Peter laughed.

"Weren't you wondering where I was?" asked Lucy. "I was hiding in the wardrobe, and the next thing I knew, I was in a wood and I met a Faun named Mr. Tumnus. I've been gone for hours!"

Peter looked at her, disbelieving. There was nothing inside the wardrobe but coats.

Peter messed up Lucy's hair.

"One game at a time, Lu." He laughed. "We don't all have your imagination."

"But I wasn't imagining!" said Lucy. "I wouldn't lie about this!"

"I believe you," said Edmund.

Lucy turned to him eagerly.

"You do?"

"Sure." He grinned. "Didn't I tell you about the football field in the bathroom cupboard?"

Peter shoved Edmund. "You just have to make everything worse, don't you?" cried Peter, angrily.

"It was a joke," said Edmund, stomping off down the hall.

"When are you going to grow up?" shouted Peter.

"Shut up! You think you're Dad, but you're not," replied Edmund.

"That was nicely handled," said Susan, quietly.

Peter sighed. He wasn't doing very well with his promise to Mum.

Later, in the middle of the night, Peter was awakened by an excited Lucy, shaking him roughly.

"Peter! Wake up!" she cried. "It's there! It's really there!"

Peter lifted himself onto his elbows.

"What are you talking about?"

"Narnia! Mr. Tumnus! It's all in the wardrobe like I told you!"

Lucy was jumping up and down.

"You've just been dreaming, Lucy," said Susan, who was awakened by all the noise.

"But I haven't," said Lucy, grinning triumphantly,

"and this time, Edmund went, too."

Peter turned to Edmund, who looked a little anxious.

Eventually, he spoke. "I was just playing along."

Peter glanced at Lucy. She seemed confused.

"But you know how little children are," Edmund went on. "They just don't know when to stop pretending."

Lucy sobbed and ran from the room. Peter glared at Edmund, then followed her out of the room, with Susan close behind.

In the hallway, they found Lucy being consoled by a kind-looking old man who Peter decided must be the Professor. Mrs. Macready was there, too, hastily wrapping her dressing gown around herself.

"Professor, I'm sorry. I told them you were not to be disturbed," she grumbled.

"It's all right, Mrs. Macready. I'm sure there's an explanation," said the Professor. He unwrapped Lucy's arms from his waist and pointed her in

Mrs. Macready's direction. "I think this one is in need of a little hot chocolate."

Lucy took Mrs. Macready's hand and went downstairs with her.

The Professor beckoned Peter and Susan to follow him.

He led them into his study. The walls were

shelved from floor to ceiling and crammed with books and ancient artifacts. There was a desk piled high with paper.

"You seem to have upset the delicate internal balance of my housekeeper," he said, looking at Peter over the top of his glasses.

"We're very sorry, sir," said Peter. "It won't happen again."

He turned to leave.

"It's Lucy, sir," said Susan.

Peter glared at her.

"The crying one?"

"Yes, sir," she continued. "She's upset."

"It's nothing," Peter said firmly. "We can handle it."

The Professor smiled. "Oh, I can see that."

Susan glanced at Peter and blurted out, "She says she's found a magical land in the upstairs wardrobe."

"What did you say?" asked the Professor, his eyes sparkling.

Peter felt very uncomfortable. "Um, the wardrobe upstairs . . . Lucy thinks she found a forest inside."

"She won't stop going on about it," added Susan.

"What was it like?"

Peter couldn't believe his ears.

"You're not saying you believe her?" he asked, incredulous. "Edmund said she was only pretending."

The Professor nodded. "And he's usually the more truthful one?"

Peter paused. "No . . . this would be the first time."

"So you think Lucy's crazy? Out of her mind, as they say?"

Susan shook her head. "I wouldn't go that far."

The Professor smiled.

"Well, if Lucy's not lying, and if she's not crazy, then logically, we must assume she's telling the truth."

"You're saying we should believe her?" Peter gawked at him. The Professor sat down and leaned toward them.

"Of course. She's your sister. You're family."

The next day it had stopped raining, so they went outside for a game of cricket.

"And Peter lines up, poised to take yet another wicket," said Peter, tossing the ball from one hand to the other.

"Can't we play hide-and-seek again?" said Edmund, sulking.

"I thought you said it was a kids' game," said Peter. "Are you ready?" he cried.

"Are *you?*" asked Edmund, with a sneer.

CHAPTER TWO

The Beavers' Dam

Peter began his run-up, whipped his arm around and bowled. Edmund gave the ball a mighty thump, hitting it high into the air. It sailed through the window of the library with a crash!

They all dashed inside. In the library, they found lots of broken glass, a collapsed suit of armor and a cricket ball lying amid the pieces.

"Well done, Ed," said Peter, trying to rebuild the suit, without much success.

"You bowled it," said Edmund, shrugging.

Peter was about to give him a piece of his mind when they heard footsteps approaching.

"The Macready!" cried Susan. They rushed out of the library and headed upstairs, leaving a very strange-looking suit of armor behind.

The footsteps followed them upstairs. Looking for somewhere to hide, Peter yanked open the wardrobe door, and they scrambled inside.

Moving coats and furs aside, Peter crawled to the back. The footsteps stopped just outside the door. He pressed back farther and suddenly felt very, very cold.

"Peter?" whispered Susan, "are your trousers wet?"

Peter looked down. He was sitting in a mound of snow.

Peter stood up and stepped out of the back of

the wardrobe. He was in a forest. Trees towered over him, their branches thick with snow. There was a lamppost in a clearing.

"Impossible!" Susan gasped.

"Don't worry," said Lucy, smartly. "I'm sure it's just your imagination."

Peter felt very, very guilty.

"I don't suppose saying we're sorry would quite cover it," he said.

"You're right," said Lucy. "It wouldn't."

She bent down, patted a handful of snow into a tight ball and whipped it into Peter's face.

"But that might!" She laughed.

Peter threw a snowball back at her, chuckling, but it sailed past and struck Edmund. The smile faded from Peter's face.

"You little liar," he said.

"You didn't believe her, either," said Edmund, defiantly.

"Apologize to Lucy," said Peter, coldly.

"All right," said Edmund, with a sneer. "I'm sorry."

Everyone knew he didn't mean it.

Lucy wanted them to meet Mr. Tumnus, the Faun. She led them through the forest toward his house.

She stopped. In front of them was a house, but its door had been ripped from its hinges. Lucy ran to it before Peter could stop her. He chased after her.

The house was a mess. Drawers had been emptied onto the floor, the crockery was smashed and the furniture was broken.

"Who would do something like this?" asked Lucy, picking up a broken teacup.

Peter lifted a piece of parchment from the floor. He read it aloud:

"The Faun Tumnus is hereby charged
with High Treason against her

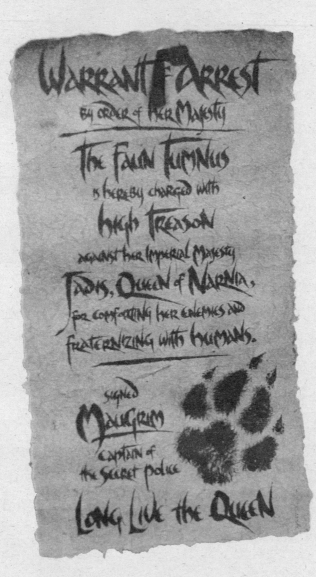

Imperial Majesty Jadis,
Queen of Narnia,
for comforting her enemies
and fraternizing with Humans.
Signed, Maugrim,
Captain of the Secret Police.
Long live the Queen."

"All right, now we really should go back," said Susan nervously.

"But what about Mr. Tumnus?" cried Lucy, turning to Peter. "I'm the Human! She must have found out he helped me."

Edmund scowled.

"Don't worry, Lu, we'll think of something," said Peter calmly.

"Why? I mean, he's a criminal. And how do we even know that the Queen's not in the right?" asked Edmund.

"Pssst!" said a voice.

Peter turned. Where had the noise come from? He stepped outside. Nothing was there.

There was a rustling in the woods. Cautiously, Peter walked toward the trees.

"Pssst!" said the voice again.

Peter pulled aside some branches. Sitting there was a very big Beaver. Peter slowly extended his hand to the creature. The Beaver put his hands upon his hips.

"I'm not going to smell it, if that's what you want," he said.

Peter's jaw dropped. "Oh, sorry," he said.

The Beaver peered at Lucy. "Lucy Pevensie?" he asked.

"Yes."

The Beaver handed her a handkerchief. Lucy stared at it.

"That's the hankie I gave to Mr. Tumnus," she

said. "Is he all right?"

The Beaver put a finger to his lips and beckoned them to follow him. He led them through
the forest until they came to a frozen river. In the
river was an enormous dam. As they got closer to
the dam, a voice called out from inside.

"Beaver? Is that you? You'd better have
brought those gooseberries I wanted."

Another Beaver stuck her head out of the
dam. Seeing the children, she dashed out of the
dam and clasped their hands.

"I never thought I'd live to see this day," she
said.

Peter was confused.

"Come inside," said Mrs. Beaver, smoothing her
fur, "and we'll see if we can't get you some food."

Peter and the others followed her into the
dam. Edmund stood a while, staring at some distant mountains, then followed miserably.

Inside, Mrs. Beaver made everyone a snack of fresh fish.

"Is there anything we can do to help Tumnus?" asked Peter.

"They have taken him to the Witch's house.

And there's few who go through those gates who ever come out again," said Mr. Beaver, shaking his head.

Lucy's eyes filled with tears. Mrs. Beaver patted her arm.

"There is hope, dear," she said.

"There's more than hope," cried Mr. Beaver. "Aslan is on the move!"

Peter stared at him, intrigued.

"Who's Aslan?" asked Edmund.

Mr. Beaver laughed. "Ha! Who's Aslan?"

He looked at their mystified faces.

"You don't know?" he asked, astonished.

"Well, we haven't been here very long," said Peter.

Mr. Beaver leaned closer.

"He's only the King of the whole wood," he said. "The real King of Narnia!"

"He's been away for a long time," said Mrs. Beaver.

"But he's back now. And he's waiting for you at the Stone Table," Mr. Beaver said.

Peter looked at Susan, completely confused.

"He's waiting for us?" Lucy smiled.

Mr. Beaver turned to his wife. "You're joking! They don't even know about the prophecy!" He turned back to the children.

"Look, Aslan's return, Tumnus's arrest, the secret police . . . It's all happening because of *you*."

"You're blaming us?" asked Susan.

"No, no. Not blaming. Thanking you," said Mrs. Beaver.

Mr. Beaver stood up. "There is a prophecy:

"When Adam's flesh and Adam's bone,
Sits at Cair Paravel in throne,
The evil time will be over and done."

"It has long been foretold that two Sons of Adam and two Daughters of Eve will defeat the

White Witch and restore peace to Narnia," added Mrs. Beaver.

Peter was silent for a moment.

"And you think we're the ones?"

"You'd better be," said Mr. Beaver.

Peter shook his head slowly. "I think you've made a mistake. We're not heroes."

"We're from Finchley," said Susan. She stood up. "Thank you for your hospitality, but we really have to go."

"What about Mr. Tumnus?" cried Lucy.

"Susan's right, Lucy. It's out of our hands," said Peter, getting to his feet. "I'm sorry, but it's time the four of us were getting home."

He turned to Edmund. "Ed?" Edmund's chair was empty.

Peter's eyes scanned the room quickly. They stopped at the front door. It was slightly open.

"I'm going to kill him," he said, through gritted teeth.

"You may not have to," said Mr. Beaver. "Has Edmund ever been to Narnia before?"

Peter and Mr. Beaver ran through the darkness, chasing Edmund's tracks through the snow. Susan and Lucy stumbled after them.

They raced on through the forest. The trail stopped at the foot of a steep cliff. Peter squinted his eyes and looked up. Far above him, he could just make out Edmund's tiny figure, climbing the sheer wall.

"Edmund!" he yelled.

"Shhh!" said Mr. Beaver. "They'll hear you!"

Peter ran to the cliff and started to climb after Edmund. Mr. Beaver grabbed his arms and dragged him from the rocks.

"Get off me!" yelled Peter.

"You're playing into her hands," said Mr. Beaver. "The Witch wants all four of you."

"Why?" cried Peter.

"To stop the prophecy from coming true. To kill you!"

Peter stopped struggling.

Mr. Beaver released him, and put a hand on his shoulder.

"Only Aslan can save your brother now."

CHAPTER THREE

Outrunning the Witch

They returned to the Beavers' house.

"Hurry, Mother. They're after us!" cried Mr. Beaver. Mrs. Beaver grabbed a basket, and Susan passed her a jar from a shelf.

"Do you think we'll need jam?" she wondered.

A ghostly howl made everyone freeze. Wolves!

"Only if the Witch serves toast," said Peter, grimly.

Mr. Beaver pulled open a door and led them all into a tunnel behind it.

"A Badger friend dug this. It comes up near his house."

"Shhh!" said Lucy, listening hard. A distant baying reached their ears. "They're in the tunnel!"

Running headlong through the tunnel, they came to a dead end.

"You should've brought a map!" Mrs. Beaver said, scolding her husband.

"There wasn't room next to the jam," replied Mr. Beaver.

Peter knelt down. Mr. Beaver jumped onto his back and pushed open a hidden hatch in the roof of the tunnel. He climbed out and helped the others climb through.

Once Peter had dusted himself off, he realized

he was in the middle of a tiny village. Woodland animals stood all around, but none moved.

"What happened here?" asked Peter.

A voice startled them all.

"This is what becomes of those who cross the Witch," said a sly-looking Fox who was leaning against a tree.

"Relax," said the Fox. "I'm one of the good guys."

Peter scrutinized the Fox for a moment before making up his mind. "What did you have in mind?"

Moments later, Peter scrambled into a tree, helping the others up behind him. No sooner were they safely hidden when a pack of Wolves tore out from the tunnel. They stopped when they saw Fox.

"Lost something, have we?" Fox asked.

"We're looking for some Humans," snarled the leading Wolf.

"Well, that's a valuable bit of information," said Fox, calmly. "Don't you think? I imagine there'd be at least a nominal reward for something like that."

A second Wolf knocked Fox to the ground and clamped his jaws around his throat.

"The reward is your life," Maugrim growled.

Fox raised his paw and pointed northward into the forest. A Wolf sniffed the trees where he pointed.

The Wolf released Fox's throat, and the pack stormed off into the forest.

Peter jumped down from the tree. Fox got to his feet and rubbed his throat.

That night, the tired group of children and animals sat quietly around a blazing campfire. Mrs. Beaver gently tended to Fox's wounds. Peter thought Fox had been incredibly brave when faced with the White Witch's fearsome Wolves.

Later, Fox was ready to be on his way. "I must gather my men. Your Majesties will need every hoof and claw in your war against the Witch," he said gravely.

"Look," replied Susan, "thank you for your help, but we're not planning on fighting any Witch."

Fox stared back at the group intently. "But

surely, your Highness . . ."

"We just want to get our brother back," confirmed Peter.

The journey through the snow was hard. They struggled to keep their feet, urged on by Mr. Beaver, who found the going much easier. After a few hours, a strange noise reached their ears. Looking behind them, Mr. Beaver's eyes were open wide.

A sleigh was bearing down upon them, travelling quickly.

"It's her!" cried Mrs. Beaver.

Mr. Beaver pointed to a small opening in the rocks to the side, and shouted to the group to hide.

They threw themselves into the snow, but it was no use. The sleigh stopped.

After some silence, Peter said, "I suppose I'll go look."

"No," said Mr. Beaver. "You're worth nothing to Narnia dead." He stuck his head above the snow and started to laugh. "Come out!" he cried. "There's someone here to see you!"

They slowly raised their heads. On the sleigh stood a tall man with a great white beard

and wearing a bright red robe. Hitched to the sleigh were eight reindeer.

"Merry Christmas, sir," said Lucy, smiling.

"It certainly is, Lucy, now that you've arrived," said Father Christmas.

"The hope you have brought us, your Majesties, is finally weakening the Witch's magic," he said. "Still . . . you could probably do with these."

He pulled a sack from his sleigh and handed a vial to Lucy. "The juice of the fireflower. One drop will cure any injury. And though I hope you never have to use it . . ." He passed Lucy a small dagger.

Susan came forward to receive her gifts, a bow with a quiver of arrows, and a horn.

"Trust in this bow and it will not easily miss," said Father Christmas. "Blow this, and wherever you are, help will come."

Next, Father Christmas withdrew a sword, a scabbard and a shield. Handing them to Peter, he

said, "The time to use these may be near at hand. Bear them well and wisely."

Peter nodded. "Thank you, sir."

Father Christmas sat back down on his seat. "Long live Aslan! And Merry Christmas," he said, cracking the reins. The reindeer took up the slack, and the sleigh moved away across the snow.

Peter looked at his sword. On it was an inscription: WHEN ASLAN BARES HIS TEETH, WINTER MEETS ITS DEATH.

Swinging it, he sliced two icicles cleanly from a branch. The forest resounded with the noise of breaking ice. Peter stared through the branches. Something was there, something . . . red.

It was a cherry tree, bursting with life.

"You know what this means?" said Peter.

"It means it's spring!" cried Lucy.

❧

When they finally reached the Great River, the surface was melting.

"We need to cross. Now!" said Peter.

"Wait, will you think about this for a minute?" asked Susan.

A howl reached them from behind.

"We don't have a minute," said Peter, grimly.

He stepped out onto the ice. It crackled. He took another step, and another. The others followed him closely.

A Wolf pack burst from the forest and surrounded them. Peter drew his sword.

"Put that down, boy. Someone could get hurt," snarled Maugrim. Peter gripped his sword tighter.

"Leave now while you can, and your brother leaves with you," said the Wolf.

"No, Peter!" cried Mr. Beaver. "Narnia needs you!"

The ice cracked again, almost toppling Peter from his feet. He lowered his sword.

Maugrim grinned. "What'll it be, son of Adam? I won't wait forever, and neither will the river."

Peter looked around. A spiderweb of cracks was spreading across the ice.

"Hold on to me!" he cried, and jammed his sword into the ice, driving it deep.

The ice shattered. The Wolves were swept downstream in a freezing torrent, yelping. Peter held tight to his sword, and his sisters held tight to him. They tumbled into the water, and Lucy stumbled up the bank. Eventually the ice righted itself with Peter and Susan still clinging to it, gasping for air. The Beavers swam to their block of ice and pushed it to shore. They dragged themselves onto solid ground, cold and wet, but safe.

As they lay there, Narnia erupted into life. Buds burst from the icy trees, tulips thrust their way through the frozen earth, and the sounds of melting snow trickled all around them. Spring was indeed coming.

Chapter Four

Aslan's Welcome

The Pevensies had finally arrived at the Stone Table. Below them was a buzzing camp. Flags flapped in the wind, and hundreds of animals busied themselves with weapons and supplies.

They made their way down to the encampment. As they entered, a hush fell. The music stopped. Animals bowed before them as they walked toward the regal tent right in the middle of the camp. An armored Centaur stood guard in front of the tent. The camp was completely silent as they stood there.

Peter lifted his sword, saluting the Centaur nervously.

"We . . . have come to see . . . Aslan," he announced. The Centaur was silent.

The tent flaps opened and out stepped an enormous, beautiful, fearsome Lion.

Lucy knelt. The Beavers bowed their heads. Peter dropped to one knee.

"Welcome, Peter, Son of Adam!" boomed Aslan. "Welcome, Susan and Lucy, Daughters of Eve."

Mr. Beaver coughed gently.

Aslan turned. "And welcome to you, Beavers. You have my thanks," he said. "But where is the fourth?"

"That's why we're here, sir," said Peter. "We need your help. Our brother's been captured by the White Witch."

"Captured?" said Aslan, raising an eyebrow.

"He betrayed them, your Majesty," said Mr. Beaver.

The Centaur stepped forward. "Then he has betrayed us all."

Aslan fixed the Centaur with a steely gaze. "Peace, Oreius!" he boomed.

The Centaur bowed and was silent once more.

"If this is true, then why does he deserve our help?" asked Aslan.

"He's our brother," said Lucy.

Aslan stared at her. "All shall be done for Edmund," he said eventually.

He moved his gaze to Peter. "But it may be harder than you think."

Aslan and Peter took a walk. They climbed back up to the ridge and looked east. Green land stretched away to a glistening sea. A castle glittered like a diamond in the distance. "That is Cair Paravel," said Aslan. "The castle of the four thrones, in one of which you must sit, Peter, as High King."

Peter stared dumbly at the view.

"You doubt the prophecy?" asked Aslan.

"No, that's just it," said Peter. "I'm *afraid* it might be true." He looked away. "Aslan, I'm not who you think I am."

Aslan looked at him. "There is a Deep Magic, more powerful than any of us, that rules all of Narnia. This Deep Magic dictates that now, as in the beginning, it must be a man who rules Narnia. And that, Son of Adam, is you."

"But I couldn't even protect my own family," said Peter, miserably.

"I will do all that I can to help your brother," said Aslan. "But I, too, want my family safe."

With that, the Great Lion turned away. Peter

gazed at the bustle of life and activity below. His concentration was only broken by the sound of a horn.

"Susan!" cried Peter, breaking into a run. Aslan followed him.

They found Susan and Lucy near the river, being attacked by Maugrim and another Wolf. Peter drew his sword and rushed to their aid. Aslan tackled the second Wolf, pinning him to the ground.

Maugrim grinned when he saw Peter approaching.

"We've already been through this, 'your Highness'," he sneered. "We both know you haven't got it in you."

Peter tightened his grip on the sword.

"You may think you're a King," said Maugrim. "But you're going to die like a dog!"

He leapt at Peter. There was a furious struggle, then all was still.

"Peter!" cried Lucy.

Maugrim's body flopped to the ground, Peter's sword buried deep in him. Peter picked himself up. Aslan released his grip on the second

Wolf. With a yelp, it vanished into the forest.

"Follow him," Aslan commanded Oreius. "He'll lead you to Edmund."

The Centaur galloped off.

"Peter, kneel," said Aslan.

Peter knelt. Aslan placed a paw on his head, let it rest there for a moment and then withdrew it.

"Rise, Sir Peter Wolf's-Bane, Knight of Narnia," said the Lion.

Peter stood. He nodded to Aslan and sheathed his sword.

It was dawn when Peter awoke. He walked from his tent into the early light, and stopped. There on the ridge was Aslan, talking with his brother, Edmund. Susan and Lucy emerged from their tent.

"Edmund!" cried Lucy, but Peter put a hand on her shoulder to calm her.

Eventually, Aslan led a shamefaced Edmund
into the camp.

"There is no need to speak to Edmund about
what has passed," Aslan said.

Lucy and Susan hugged their brother. Peter

stared at him, hiding his relief.

At breakfast, Peter told his brother and sisters they should go home, but that he had promised Aslan that he would stay and help. But Edmund insisted that they must all stay.

"I've seen what the Witch can do—I helped her do it, and I'm not leaving these people behind to suffer for it."

"I guess that's it, then," said Susan, standing to pick up her bow.

"Where are you going?" asked Peter.

"To get in some practice."

Susan and Lucy concentrated on target practice with their bow and dagger, while Peter and Edmund had lessons in fighting on horseback. Edmund's mount was a brown Horse named Philip, while Peter's steed was a beautiful white Unicorn.

They had spent the whole morning trying to

master their weapons, when Mr. Beaver rushed into their midst, almost getting run over by Edmund's Horse.

"The Witch has demanded a meeting with Aslan!" he cried. "She's on her way here!"

Horns echoed around the camp.

The Witch was carried into camp on a bier by four Cyclopses. They stopped in front of Aslan's tent and set her down. She smiled.

Aslan waited silently beneath his flag, Peter and the others behind him.

"You have a traitor amongst you, Aslan," said the Witch at last.

Edmund closed his eyes and swallowed.

"His offense was not against you," said Aslan.

"Have you forgotten the laws upon which Narnia is built?" asked the Witch, her eyes flashing.

Aslan growled. "Do not cite the Deep Magic to me, Witch. I was there when it was written."

The Witch leaned forward. "Then you know that every traitor belongs to me."

Lucy gasped. Peter gripped his sword.

The Witch pointed at Edmund. "His blood is my property!"

CHAPTER FIVE

The Battle for Narnia Begins

Peter drew his sword from its scabbard and stepped in front of Edmund.

"Try and take him," he yelled.

The Witch barely glanced at Peter.

"Do you really think mere force can deny me

my rights . . . little King?"

She shifted her gaze to the Lion. "Aslan knows that unless I have blood, as the law demands, all of Narnia will be overturned and perish in fire and water."

Aslan stared at her, his eyes burning.

"You dare not refuse me," said the White Witch.

"What you say is true." Aslan sighed.

"It can't be true!" cried Lucy. "How can it be right to give Edmund to her?"

"I didn't say it was right," said Aslan, sadly.

"You said you'd help him!" Lucy protested. "You said he was safe!"

Aslan fixed his eyes upon the Witch again.

"I shall talk with you alone," he growled.

He walked into his tent. The Witch followed.

They were in there for some time. Peter sat on the grass and stared at the door of the tent. When the flap moved, he leapt back to his feet. Aslan and the Witch emerged, the Witch beaming.

Aslan was silent for a moment, then he looked at Peter.

"She has renounced her claim on your brother's blood," he said.

Peter punched Edmund on the arm. Edmund opened his mouth, but no sound came out. The Witch remounted her bier and was carried out of camp, followed by hisses and jeers from Aslan's army.

Aslan padded slowly back into his tent.

Later, Peter and Edmund were fast asleep when a flutter of green leaves whistled into their tent, waking them both. Peter sat bolt upright in bed. The leaves formed themselves into a woman's shape.

"Be still, my Princes," said the woman. "I bring grave news from your sisters."

And so it was that Peter and Edmund learned

with horror that Aslan, the Great Lion, had died at the hands of the White Witch.

Soon after, Peter walked slowly from the tent. He shook his head. "She's right. He's gone."

"Then you'll have to lead us. There's an army out there ready to follow you, Peter," Edmund said.

"I can't!" said Peter, despairing. He looked up. His eyes were red.

"Aslan obviously believed you could," replied Edmund, putting his hand on Peter's shoulder. "And so do I."

Peter stepped out of the tent and spoke to Oreius.

"What are your orders, sire?" asked the Centaur. Peter looked down at the battle map with a determined look in his eyes. The army would meet the White Witch in battle . . . without Aslan.

The army advanced as dawn broke over Narnia. Peter rode his Unicorn ahead of hundreds of troops marching in file.

When the troops had reached their stations, they stopped and waited nervously. A Gryphon cried high in the sky, then swooped down through the air toward Peter.

"They come, your Highness," said the Gryphon. "In numbers and weapons far greater than our own."

"Numbers do not win a battle," said Oreius.

"No, but I bet they help," replied Peter.

Peter could hear the trumpets and thunderous hooves of the White Witch's army approaching.

The army answered with a war cry that made Peter grin from ear to ear. He lifted his sword in a salute to his soldiers, then deliberately turned and pointed it at the White Witch. She sat in a chariot pulled by polar bears.

"I'm not interested in prisoners!" said the White Witch coldly. "Kill them all!"

Her army charged in an ominous thunder of hooves and steel. Peter waited, sword held high.

As they drew nearer, he lowered it until it pointed dead ahead.

"For Narnia, and for Aslan!" he yelled, spurring his Unicorn to a full gallop.

The two armies met in a crunching, shuddering noise as talons, claws, swords and lances collided. Peter rode his Unicorn through the carnage, heading for the White Witch. All around him, Ogres,

Fauns and Centaurs fought desperately. Arrows hailed down from the ridge where Edmund was directing their fire.

At last, Peter found himself heading straight for the Witch's chariot. Her polar bears snarled as they pounded through the fighting. The Witch's evil Dwarf Ginarrbrik shot an arrow straight at Peter's brave Unicorn. He stumbled and collapsed heavily. Then, suddenly, Peter found himself toppling to the ground. When he picked himself up, he was surrounded by Ogres. The White Witch strode toward him. Peter hacked and slashed with his sword to keep the Ogres at bay, but all the time the Witch came nearer, her wand ready to turn him to stone. She raised it high, pointed it at Peter and smiled.

The smile was replaced by a twisted snarl as Edmund's sword sliced clean through the wand.

Edmund fell to the ground, exhausted by his dash from the ridge. The Witch turned to him,

slashing with the half of her wand she still held. He tried to roll clear, but the Witch stabbed him in the side with the wand. Edmund groaned and lay motionless.

"No!" shouted Peter. He finished off the last Ogre and charged at the Witch in a fury. He swung his sword desperately, the Witch parrying and lunging with her broken wand. Peter felt his feet slip on the loose gravel beneath him, and found himself on his back, with the Witch standing above him. She drew back her wand to deliver the killing blow when a mighty roar shook the very earth beneath them all.

It was the roar of a Great Lion.

CHAPTER SIX

Peter's Destiny

The Witch stopped. She looked at the ridge, her face dark with fear. Peter followed her gaze. There on the ridge was the figure of a huge Lion. It was joined by a thousand other creatures, all silhouetted against the sun.

The Witch's army gave a great cry of fear and turned to run.

The Witch faced Peter, hatred in her eyes. She knocked his sword from his hands and kicked him viciously in the head. Peter looked up at her smiling face, wondering if this was his end. A low growl from behind made the Witch look up, and fear replaced the hatred in her eyes.

"Impossible," she whispered.

A great golden form leapt over Peter and pounced on the Witch. A mighty roar rang out. Peter looked away.

"It is done," said a familiar voice.

Peter turned. It was Aslan.

"Peter!" cried a voice.

Peter turned to see Susan and Lucy running across the battlefield toward him. They ran into his arms, and he hugged them.

"Where's Edmund?" asked Lucy, looking around.

Tears welled in Peter's eyes.

Susan spotted him first.

"Edmund!" she yelled.

He lay where he had fallen, still clutching the wand stuck in his side. They ran to him.

As they neared him, a Dwarf dragged himself to his feet. He picked up an axe and stood over Edmund. The Dwarf raised the axe above his head.

"Down!" cried Susan, grabbing her bow and an arrow from her quiver. Peter and Lucy dropped to the ground. Susan took sight and released the arrow. It flew straight and true, piercing the Dwarf between the shoulder blades. The Dwarf fell.

They finally reached their brother. Susan cradled his head. Lucy pulled the vial from her clothes and let one glistening drop splash onto Edmund's lips. His ragged breath became more regular. His eyes opened. He smiled. Lucy hugged him tight.

Aslan stalked the battlefield, breathing on

each creature that had been turned to stone by the Witch. As his breath touched them, they came back to life.

Many hours later, when Lucy had tended to the wounded, and Aslàn had turned his breath on the Witch's last victims, the Great Lion led them to Cair Paravel.

In the Great Hall were four stone thrones. One had a sword carved into it, one a horn, another a tiny bottle and the last a wand, broken in two. Peter, Susan, Edmund and Lucy stood before them, awed. The hall was filled with Narnians, gazing happily on their new rulers.

Peter sat upon his throne. The doors at the far end of the hall opened and in strode Aslan. The Narnians parted to allow him to approach the thrones.

Mr. Tumnus pinned a silver laurel into Lucy's hair. The Faun smiled.

"In the name of the Eastern Sea," said Aslan in a grave voice, "I give you Queen Lucy, the Valiant."

Oreius the Centaur placed a silver crown on Edmund's head.

"In the name of the Western Woods, King Edmund, the Just," said Aslan.

Mrs. Beaver perched a ring of golden flowers on Susan's hair.

"In the name of the Radiant Southern Sun, Queen Susan, the Gentle."

Mr. Tumnus rested a heavy golden crown on Peter's bowed head.

Aslan raised his voice just a little. "And in the name of Clear Northern Sky, I give you King Peter, the Magnificent. May you rule long, Kings and Queens of Narnia, and may your wisdom grace us until the stars rain down from the heavens."

After the ceremony, there was a great celebration. The Narnians danced with their new Kings and Queens and celebrated the end of winter and the start of a new age.

The years passed. The Kings and Queens of Narnia grew into wise and noble rulers.

Many years later, they found themselves out riding in the woods and came upon the most unusual sight. Instead of the usual trees and bushes, in the middle of the clearing was a lamppost.

"By the Lion's Mane," declared Peter. "What is this?"

"It runs in my mind, too," said Lucy. "As if in a dream."

They dismounted, each examining the lamppost curiously. A White Stag suddenly burst across the clearing and galloped into the forest. On foot, Peter chased it.

The wood was very dark. They felt their way with arms outstretched.

"I feel strange," said Edmund.

"These are not branches," murmured Peter.

"They're . . . coats?" said Lucy.

They pushed their way through the darkness until they tumbled to the floor, just outside the wardrobe in Professor Kirke's house. Memories crowded Peter's mind.

Professor Kirke entered the room.

"Oh, I'm sorry," he said. "I didn't know you were in here."

He gazed at them, sitting on the floor in front of his wardrobe.

"What were you all doing in the wardrobe?" he asked.

Peter sighed. "You would not believe us if we told you, sir."

The others giggled.

The Professor smiled and tossed a cricket ball to Peter.

"Try me," he said, his eyes twinkling.

EXCERPT FROM
Lucy's Adventure: The Search for Aslan
Adapted by Michael Flexer

CHAPTER ONE

Lucy Steps Through the Wardrobe

Lucy Pevensie was only eight years old, but she still knew a lot of things. She wasn't completely sure why she was standing on the platform of a train station with her two brothers, Peter and Edmund, and her sister, Susan, but she knew it had something to do with the War. Daddy had gone to fight people called the Nazis, who were turning Europe into a horrible and dangerous place. Even though fighting is a bad thing to do, Lucy understood that it was important sometimes to fight to save and protect the innocent and the good. What Lucy didn't understand was why the Nazis were dropping bombs on people's houses in London and making her leave her mother behind and go into the countryside. That, Lucy couldn't understand.

As her mother hugged her, Lucy thought that it didn't seem very fair. If it wasn't safe for her and her brothers and sister to live in London anymore, then how could it be safe for their mother? Lucy grabbed hold of her older brother Peter's hand. He was practically a grown-up like Mummy and Daddy anyway. As they stepped onto the train that would take them to their new home, the home of Professor Kirke, Lucy turned to wave good-bye to her mother and watched sadly as she followed the train down the platform.

The long train ride to the country ended at an empty platform. An old black buggy pulled up and a very stern woman got out. Lucy felt very small indeed under the woman's glare.

"Mrs. . . . Macready?" Peter stammered.

"I'm afraid so," came the reply.

Lucy felt even smaller upon seeing the Professor's mansion. As the others followed Mrs. Macready down the hall, Lucy stopped. A light had just flickered behind a nearby door. Suddenly, a shadow moved underneath it. Lucy gasped and dashed away to catch up with the others.

"The covers feel scratchy."

Lucy didn't like her new home. She didn't like the scary Mrs. Macready who had met them at the train station. She didn't like the dark staircases.

She didn't like the way the floor felt cold and unfriendly underneath her bare feet. And she didn't like her new bed. The new bed was the worst of all, but it wasn't really the covers that upset Lucy. It was the fact that her mother wasn't there to tuck her in at night and tell her everything was going to be okay.

Susan tried to comfort Lucy, "Wars don't last forever, Lucy. We'll be home soon."

"If home's still there," replied Edmund.

This was too much for Lucy. She didn't want to think of her lovely home being turned into a pile of burnt bricks. Lucy felt tears in her eyes.

Peter smiled and tried to cheer them all up. "Tomorrow's going to be great."

But it wasn't great at all. It was just very, very, very rainy.

Inside, all four children were bored. Susan was trying to make them play a dictionary game.

Lucy loved her sister, but thought that sometimes she could be a bit boring. Susan didn't seem to like outdoor games, but Lucy loved them. She liked running around and playing the games her brothers played. She wasn't afraid of exploring in forests or climbing trees or going to strange places.

"We could play hide-and-seek," Lucy suggested.

"Hide-and-seek's for children," Edmund said. He was only a little older than Lucy, and always tried to act more grown-up than he was. Lucy didn't mind. She knew that Peter would play. Peter sighed and looked up into Lucy's pleading face. "One," he said slowly. "Two, three . . ."

Lucy darted away.

Lucy dashed toward the windows and ripped back a heavy velvet curtain.

"I was here first," Edmund said, snapping the curtain back into place. Hurrying down the hall, Lucy came to a closed door.

"Eighty-nine," Peter said.

Quickly, Lucy shoved open the door and went inside. The room was empty except for a large wardrobe that sat against the wall. She hurried over to it and yanked on the knob. Taking a deep breath, Lucy dived into the wardrobe.

Inside, it was dark and surprisingly cold, as if there was a wind. Lucy decided to hide deep among the coats, so she put out her hand to feel for the back of the wardrobe. It seemed to be a very big wardrobe, and Lucy had to really stretch and stretch and then she felt something. . . .

"Ouch!"

Lucy frowned. That was strange—she had touched something prickly. Why would there be something prickly in the wardrobe?

She took a step forward. *Crunch.*

What is that? Lucy wondered. Feeling strangely colder, she crunched her way through the darkness. Lucy couldn't believe how big the wardrobe

was and how cold and how prickly the coats were. Ahead of her, there was a tiny dot of very bright light. Lucy took another step into the impossibly big wardrobe. Slowly, the darkness around her lifted and everything was bathed in light. Then Lucy saw that the coat she had been touching was no coat at all but a green tree branch. She was standing in a forest . . . and it was snowing. There was a lamppost in the clearing in front of her.

Something crunched in the snow behind Lucy. She turned quickly and saw a very strange creature. He had legs like a goat, and two horns growing out of a thick patch of curly hair on his head. He was wearing a red scarf and carried an umbrella in one hand, and a bunch of packages wrapped in brown paper in the other.

The creature and Lucy let out a scream at the same time. The goat-man hopped behind a tree. Lucy was frightened, but she didn't know what to do.

"Are you hiding from me?" Lucy asked.

The creature peeped out from behind the tree. "No . . ." he said slowly, "I was just . . . I didn't want to scare you."

"If you don't mind me asking . . . what are you?" Lucy inquired. She was scared but she knew the creature was more frightened than she was.

"I'm a Faun! What about you? Are you some kind of beardless Dwarf?" the goat-man asked.

Lucy laughed. "I'm not a Dwarf," she told him. "I'm a girl!"

The creature gaped at her. "You're Human?"

"Of course," Lucy said.

The creature glanced around nervously as though he was expecting someone to arrive.

"I'm sorry. Allow me to introduce myself. My name is Tumnus."

"Pleased to meet you, Mr. Tumnus. I'm Lucy Pevensie." Lucy thought that Fauns weren't real, but she didn't want to upset Mr. Tumnus, so she kept quiet. After all, for an imaginary creature, he did seem very friendly.

"Well then, Lucy Pevensie . . . how would it be if you came and had tea with me?" asked the Faun shyly.

Lucy told Mr. Tumnus that she ought to be getting back, but he wouldn't take no for an answer. "We'll have a roaring fire," he promised, "and toast and hot tea and cake."

OWN A WORLD OF ADVENTURE
ON DISNEY DVD SPRING 2006!

WALT DISNEY PICTURES AND WALDEN MEDIA
PRESENT
-THE CHRONICLES OF-
NARNIA
THE LION, THE WITCH AND THE WARDROBE